The Doomsday Date

I am a reader and I celebrated World Book Day 2024
with this gift from my local bookseller
and Usborne Publishing

WORLD BOOK DAY's mission is to offer every child and young person the opportunity to read and love books by giving you the chance to have a book of your own.

To find out more, and for fun activities including video stories, audiobooks and book recommendations, visit **WORLDBOOKDAY.COM**

World Book Day® is a charity sponsored by National Book Tokens.

Also by FARIDAH ÀBÍKÉ-ÍYÍMÍDÉ:

ACE OF SPADES

WHERE SLEEPING GIRLS LIE

Coming soon:

FOUR EIDS AND A FUNERAL

(with ADIBA JAIGIRDAR)

The Doomsday Date

FARIDAH ÀBÍKÉ-ÍYÍMÍDÉ

USBORNE

*For my sister Tamera, who reminds me every day
how ancient I am, having been born in the 90s*

First published in the UK in 2024 by Usborne Publishing Limited, Usborne House,
83-85 Saffron Hill, London EC1N 8RT, England, usborne.com

Usborne Verlag, Usborne Publishing Limited, Prüfeninger Str. 20, 93049 Regensburg,
Deutschland, VK Nr. 17560

Text copyright © Faridah Àbíké-Íyímídé, 2024

The right of Faridah Àbíké-Íyímídé to be identified as the author of this work has been
asserted by her in accordance with the Copyright, Designs and Patents Act, 1988.

Cover illustration by Bex Glendining © Usborne Publishing, 2024

Photograph of Faridah Àbíké-Íyímídé © Joy Olugboyega

The name Usborne and the Balloon logo are Trade Marks of
Usborne Publishing Limited

A CIP catalogue record for this book is available from the British Library.

ISBN 9781805076483   9612/1   JFMAMJJASO D/23

Printed and bound using 100% renewable energy at CPI Group (UK) Ltd,
Croydon, CR0 4YY.

World Book Day® and the associated logo are the registered
trademarks of World Book Day® Limited.
Registered charity number 1079257 (England and Wales).
Registered company number 03783095 (UK)

A brief note on the historical setting of this book:

Our story takes place long, long ago; in an ancient time when dinosaurs roamed the aisles of old Blockbuster stores; when mobile phones were still the size of large blocks of cheese. A time before modern inventions such as Instagram, TikTok and sliced bread. When keeping your Tamagotchi[1] alive was a main priority. When *scary spice* was in fact a person and not just another name for chilli paste. And when wearing outfits comprised solely of denim was seen as a perfectly sound choice to make and not at all a cry for help. What time was

---

[1] Old-timey gaming device

this, you ask? The 1990s, of course.

And it was during this ancient time when arguably one of the most important historical events ever came about, at midnight on the 31st December 1999: the end of the world.

Or, rather: the day the world was *meant* to end.

As you can probably tell from the fact that the earth is still somewhat intact[2], the world did not cease to exist on the 1st January 2000. However, given the fact that millions and millions of people around the world sat with bated breath, waiting impatiently for the world to explode, it is safe to say that the 31st December 1999 was a pretty intense day.

And that's where this story starts. With one of the people who truly believed that the world would end that fateful Friday, many centuries[3] ago.

---

[2] FYI climate change is real and we need to take action fast.
[3] Twenty-five years ago

31st December 1999

On the day before the world was meant to end, Sanjeet Joshi dyed his hair pink.

He wasn't quite sure why – pink was never a colour he'd particularly liked – but it was on the *Doomsday bucket list* he'd created weeks before. And he'd promised his past self that he'd complete every single weird task on the list. Including dyeing his hair.

So far he'd already eaten sweets for breakfast (which he never usually did), smoked his first (and last) cigarette (which tasted like the grim reaper's sweat, by the way), and ridden his bike without wearing his helmet.

He'd done four out of the ten things on his list, and he was determined to do them *all* by midnight…even the last one. The one that scared him the most. The one he'd sworn he'd never do, unless it was a life-or-death situation. And, well, now it apparently was.

The apocalypse was coming – or as some were calling it, the Y2K bug. When the clock ticked from 11.59 p.m. on the 31st December 1999 to 12 a.m. on the 1st January 2000, computer systems were going to fail while planes fell from the sky, the world was going to explode and everyone was going to die.

This was what Sanjeet believed, along with millions of others around the world.

The Y2K bug would kill them all, and there was nothing he could do about it but live his last day to the fullest.

Sola Akindele didn't believe in conspiracies. Especially not the ridiculous ones her best friend and next-door neighbour Sanjeet believed.

When they were five, she'd had to break the news to him about both Santa Claus and the tooth fairy – which he hadn't taken so well.

When they were ten, she'd stayed up with him when he thought there was a UFO outside his window, ready to abduct him and snatch him away from his friends and family for ever. Turned out the "UFO" was just a Frisbee stuck to the lamp post.

Now that they were sixteen, Sola hoped that by distracting Sanjeet with his strange bucket list, when midnight *did* come around and the world didn't explode, he'd come to his senses and stop letting his imagination play tricks on him.

One might ask how such different people came to be best friends. Sola: the mellow and unafraid cynic who hated people and life, and generally kept to herself at school, blending into the shadows. And Sanjeet: the lively but anxious boy-next-door, who loved life and people. But the answer was simple, really. Born on the same day, in the same hospital, with mums who were also the best of friends – it was literally written in the stars. The two were practically made for each other.

There was no Sola without Sanjeet, in the same way that the solar system could not exist without the sun.

They'd known each other since before they could form words or walk properly. They'd taken more bubble baths together than Sanjeet would like to admit, and they told each other everything.

Well, *almost* everything.

They were each other's favourite person, and even though Sola would do and say things that made Sanjeet even more anxious, and Sanjeet's conspiracies made Sola want to gouge her eyes out, they loved each other more than words could express.

Sola sometimes suspected that she loved him a little more than she was meant to… And that was why, instead of being at home, reading another Octavia E. Butler novel in the comfort of her own room, she was in the very tidy dungeon[4] that was Sanjeet's bedroom, coating his now-bleached hair with copious amounts of pink hair dye.

When she'd received his SOS call that morning – aka rocks thrown at her bedroom window at the crack of dawn – and he'd told her about his bucket list, she'd suspected he'd finally lost it. However, as Sola had watched him eat gummy worms for breakfast, ride his bike like a hyperactive kid through their neighbourhood, and choke on the toxic fumes of the cigarette he'd been keeping hidden away in his room specially for today, she didn't suspect it any more. It was confirmed.

Sanjeet had completely lost the plot.

---

[4] Not an actual dungeon, Sanjeet's bedroom just happened to be in the basement.

Never in her life had she imagined Sanjeet dyeing his hair, let alone bright pink. It seemed like today, anything was possible. Who knew, maybe he'd invent time travel next?

She wondered what else he had on that ridiculous list of his.

"Be honest," Sanjeet started, once they'd washed the dye out of his hair. "Do I look bad?"

Sola inspected his face, taking in the drastic way the pink stood out against his dark-brown skin. She tried to ignore the way her heart jolted a little as he stared up at her from his seat on the bed.

He looked like a rock star.

But she'd never admit that out loud.

"Honestly? Yes," she lied. She didn't like lying to him, but sometimes it was necessary.

Sanjeet sighed, grabbing a folded-up sheet of paper from the pocket of his hoodie and ticking *Dye my hair pink* off the list.

"Thanks. At least I'll die knowing pink isn't my colour."

Sola forced a smile.

"At least there's that," she said, ignoring the dread in the pit of her stomach.

She felt like something was coming, something that could change everything. Not the end of the world, but something else…something bigger, and she wasn't sure if that was a good thing.

"I look like one of those creepy trolls your mum used to collect," he said, squinting at himself in the mirror.

Maybe that's why it's sort of endearing, Sola thought to herself. Her mum used to collect all sorts of things: strange mugs with bright graphics, rainbow shoelaces and wrinkly trolls with neon-coloured hair. They were practically all Sola had inherited.

When Sola's mum had died four years ago, she and her older brother, Tobi, had been left with their tiny house – and the bills and rent that needed to be paid, which Tobi, in his big-brotherly fashion, dealt with via his many part-time jobs – as well as a whole box of really pointless things.

"Hey! Don't insult the trolls, they look *way* better than you do," she said, which made Sanjeet raise an eyebrow at her.

Sensing that an object could be flying her way any moment, Sola braced herself to duck.

"Well, not all of us are models like you, Sola. Some of us have to get by on being charming and hilarious."

Sola smiled, her stomach doing that annoying twisting motion again.

"True. So since you're not charming or hilarious, what do you have going for you?"

Sanjeet grabbed his pillow and tossed it at Sola's head.

"My aim," he said, smile as bright as his hair.

Number five on the Doomsday bucket list:

Learn how to skateboard.

(Or at least try to without dying. Not that it'd matter much with the whole Y2K apocalypse thing.)

The bucket list found them this time inside the belly of a pigeon – more specifically Pigeon Park, aka the public gardens down the hill from where they both lived. And even more specifically, in the centre of the park, in what locals nicknamed *the belly* (mostly because the floral arrangements around the park formed the shape of a bird and so the middle of the park was thought to be the pigeon's stomach).

Sola wasn't quite sure that she agreed with that assessment, especially as stomachs didn't tend to be in the centre of the body. It would be more accurate to say they were in the pigeon's intestines.

In fact, she'd prefer it.

Sanjeet had been standing on the skateboard in the pigeon's large intestines for a while now, eyes closed, legs shaky.

To the outside observer, it might have seemed like this was not a big achievement, but to Sanjeet, it was. They'd been at this for half an hour, trying to get him to balance, and while he wasn't exactly *skateboarding*, he at least hadn't fallen, cracked his head open and died.

(Yet.)

"Okay, I'm going to try to move," he said.

"Sure," Sola replied.

"I'm going to do it."

"Mm-hmm."

"Any minute now…" he said.

Sola looked at him sideways. "Sure you don't want me to help you along?"

Sanjeet shook his head. "That'd be cheating, I have to do this alone."

He took a deep breath, staying completely still, while praying to the universe that he'd be okay, that this wasn't going to kill him.

Then he shifted back a little and, as he felt the world move from under him and his life flash before his eyes, he did what any person on the brink of death would do and screamed.

"Did I do it?" he yelled.

"Kind of…" Sola replied.

He did the same thing again, and moved a bit more, yelling "Oh god!" as he felt the board shift beneath him.

He opened his eyes, expecting to be at least a few metres away from Sola, but it was almost like he hadn't moved at all.

Sola was seated on the park bench, watching him with the smile she only ever gave him.

She was finding this funny.

He pulled his bucket list from his pocket and gave the spot where it read *Learn how to skateboard* a reluctant tick, before pocketing it once again.

"If I had more time, I'd be a pro at it...Tony Hawk-level good."

"Sure," Sola said, grin getting wider.

Sanjeet felt his stomach turn. He checked his watch. It was already 5.30 p.m.; he only had a few hours left to complete his bucket list and say goodbye to everyone for good.

He thought about what it would mean to have to say goodbye, to never see his mum or dad or his sister Anika again. The end of all the things he loved most, like the crisp pappadums his dad always picked up from the grocery store for teatime, or his mum's smoky chicken biryani and warm chapatis.

His eyes met Sola's.

No more sneaking over next door to hang out and stay up playing video games. Or watching Sola's favourite old movies and dancing badly to her latest pop-song obsession in the living room.

No more Sola...

"You hungry?" Sanjeet asked Sola, pushing the bad thoughts and the anxieties that came with them away.

"Always," she replied.

It was dinner time in the Joshi household. Sanjeet and Sola were seated around the oval walnut-coloured table in the cosy nest of the dining room with Sanjeet's sister, mum and dad. His mum had made an assortment of dishes, which were spread across the table in bowls. The smell alone would have been enough to lure them back home from their adventures outside, but there was also the fact that Sanjeet's mum did not like it when he was late to dinner and so he always rushed back to avoid a lengthy lecture about timekeeping.

In some parallel universe maybe this truly was

one of their last meals – in which case, Sola was glad it was this. Nothing beat Mrs Joshi's chicken biryani or Mr Joshi's home-made chai.

"Sanjeet, you're not eating…" Sanjeet's mum said, after watching him shovel food up and down his mostly untouched plate. Sola was already onto seconds.

"I, umm, had a big lunch," Sanjeet lied. He hadn't had any lunch thus far, or a real breakfast. The only things he'd consumed had been sweets, half a cigarette and probably the fumes from his hair dye – which his parents hadn't commented on, presumably because they, like Sola, assumed he was going through a quarter-life crisis.

The real reason why Sanjeet wasn't eating his mum's incredibly delicious food was because of number six on the list.

"Oh, well then, you should still try to eat. You can't grow if you don't eat good food," his mum said, while his dad nodded vigorously. Sanjeet's mum was a nurse, and Sanjeet's parents were suspicious of all processed things.

"It's true. Your mum's right, growth is important," Sola replied with a mouth half full of rice.

"Thank you for talking sense into him, my dear," Sanjeet's mum said warmly to Sola, who had become as much of a member of the Joshi family as Sanjeet over the years.

Sanjeet squinted his eyes at Sola as he begrudgingly shoved a large spoonful of rice into his mouth. She squinted back teasingly, and then grinned, exposing her wide rice-riddled teeth.

"Do you enjoy being a menace to society or does it just come naturally to you?" Sanjeet asked, as they found their coats so they could head out into the cold late-December air once again.

"A bit of both," Sola replied. She slipped on her

brother's padded denim jacket – which was basically hers now seeing as she'd borrowed the jacket many moons ago and had never got around to returning it. "I guess it's payback for the time you killed my Tamagotchi," she said.

Sanjeet tried to look innocent as they made their way out the door. "I have no idea what you're talking about."

"Convenient," Sola said with a smile, nudging him softly as they walked along the path to their next stop.

Number six on the Doomsday bucket list:

Eat fast food for the first time.

(preferably a combo of a burger and fries)

Because of his parents' love of home-made food, Sanjeet had never had any sweets or chocolates (especially not for breakfast) and he'd never *ever* eaten fast food before.

He'd spent years watching Sola inhale an impossible number of hamburgers, without ever actually trying one. But on the 31st December 1999, that was going to change.

Sola slid into one of the booths at the only American diner in town, formally known as The Parlour and informally referred to by Sanjeet's parents as The Diner of Death. Upon first glance, there was nothing seemingly special or unique about the diner; however, once inside, the reason for its name immediately became clear. The decor was set up like an actual old-fashioned parlour. There were pictures of the owner's family hanging on the beige wallpapered walls of the diner, floral-patterned armchairs in place of dining chairs and mismatched plates, cups and furnishings to drive home the cosy English home-made theme, which was at odds with the American diner food they served.

Sola loved The Parlour, not only because of the way it looked and felt inside, but also because it was the one place she, her mum and her brother would always go to whenever they wanted to have a special meal or outing. Having a family holiday was never financially feasible, so this was their treat instead – usually twice a month and on birthdays.

Seeing as Sola was the expert and Sanjeet a novice in this department, Sanjeet put Sola in charge of the ordering.

"Here we are: two super-stacked burgers with a side of chunky chips." Sola arrived back with their tray of "goods".

Sola immediately got to work, diving straight into her cheeseburger.

The smell of fried food wafted into Sanjeet's nose. He wasn't sure if it was because he'd ended up eating a whole plate of rice under his mother's watchful eye, or if it was the fact that the burger looked as though it had been dowsed in a bucket of oil, but he was starting to feel queasy.

Maybe his parents did have a point when they called this place The Diner of Death.

He stared at his bucket list open on his lap in front of him. The list might have seemed like it was filled with trivial things, but each item served a very specific purpose, acting as a constant reminder of why it was important he completed this challenge.

Sanjeet was only sixteen, but he felt as though

he'd wasted his entire life before today.

He'd hardly ever taken any risks or done anything truly exciting. He lived life by the book, and what for? So that he could die never having lived?

The thought of that scared him more than anything on this list.

Well, almost anything.

He picked up the burger, surprised by how heavy it was (probably because of all the gunk it was filled with).

Then he looked at Sola, who had finished her own cheeseburger and was now eyeing the one in his hands.

"I'm only taking a bite, you can have the rest," Sanjeet said, and her eyes lit up, which made him happy. Seeing Sola doing most things made him happy – even watching her fall asleep made him happy. Which sounded creepy, but Sanjeet swore it wasn't.

It was just that best-friend thing, when you feel connected in a way you don't feel with anyone else.

Sanjeet squeezed his eyes shut and bit into the burger, immediately regretting his decision as he began to chew and taste the flavours.

He dumped the rest onto Sola's tray, wiping his mouth with the napkin.

"I'm guessing you didn't like it?" Sola said, immediately taking a bite out of his abandoned burger.

"Tasted like cat piss," Sanjeet said, still pulling a face.

"How do you know what cat piss tastes like…?" Sola asked, eyebrows raised.

"What I *assume* it would taste like."

"Sure…"

"I don't drink cat piss," he whispered.

"And I believe you." Sola thew him a mischievous glance.

"Whatever. You can enjoy the cat urine burger,

while I try to get this taste out of my mouth."

Sola grabbed the bucket list from his lap. "Well, trying a fizzy drink *is* next on your list," she said. "So you can try mine if you need something to wash away the taste."

Sanjeet's eyes widened and he snatched the bucket list back. "Why'd you take that?" he asked, shoving it back into his pocket.

Sola paused, staring at him. "It was on your lap—"

"Doesn't mean you should take it," he snapped. "It's private."

Sola went quiet for a few moments. She hadn't even seen anything past number seven... What was he hiding?

"Aren't we completing the list together anyway? Shouldn't I know what weird thing you want me to help you with next?"

Sanjeet said nothing, just stared at the table in silence.

"What's so private that you can't tell me? I thought we told each other everything…" Sola asked quietly.

More silence.

"Hello? Earth to Sanjeet Joshi," she said, waving her hands in his face.

"If you think this is weird and pointless, you don't have to help me, you know. I'm not holding a gun to your head. You can leave, you don't have to follow me everywhere. I can handle a simple list by myself," Sanjeet said harshly.

Sola's face dropped and she gave him a look she'd given him just once before, when he'd accidentally spilled tea all over one of the only pictures she had of herself with her mum, partially destroying the photo in the process.

It was a look that was rare because Sola hardly ever got angry. She didn't let herself care enough about things to get angry, especially when it concerned Sanjeet. But maybe it was because being in The Parlour always brought up old memories of her mum, or because she'd put up with his annoying ramblings about Doomsday and his self-indulgence all year (as she'd known he was in an anxious spiral). But now he was snapping at her and she'd finally had enough.

She took her drink and pushed it towards him, shoving it a little too hard, which sent it spilling onto the table.

"Number seven," she said, standing up. "You can finish your bucket list alone and spend the rest of Doomsday alone too for all I care. You clearly don't want me here and so I won't be bothering you any more. Goodbye, Sanjeet."

"Sola—" he started, but she didn't let him finish.

"Oh, and if the world does end tonight, I guess I'll see you in hell," she said, before grabbing her bag and leaving the restaurant.

Sanjeet had royally messed up.

Which might have been the understatement of the decade.

Not only had he pissed off Sola on the day he needed her most, he'd also managed to stick a needle into the wrong part of his ear, which, as expected, caused a significant amount of blood loss and resulted in him fainting.

Today should not have gone like this.

Sanjeet hadn't meant to spend his final day on earth alone on his bathroom floor with blood pooling from his ear.

And yet here he was.

Number eight on Sanjeet's list was to get a piercing, and he'd been hoping Sola would help him with that, but he hadn't anticipated her dumping him today.

As he stared up at the ceiling, blood trickling down his neck, he thought about how patient Sola always was with him, and how he threw that right back in her face today. He truly deserved the award for the world's worst best friend.

To make matters worse, the odds were that Sola could be right about the end of the world. Sola tended to be right about a lot of things, meaning he ruined one of the only good things in his life for no reason.

She was right about him being a bad friend, so maybe she'd been right about him being irrational too.

Maybe the world wasn't ending.

Maybe he ate that piss burger and made himself look like a pink-haired troll and stuck a needle in his ear for nothing.

Whether or not she was right about Doomsday though, he had to fix their friendship and fast.

After all, he *could* be right, the world could be ending. And the last thing he wanted to do was spend an eternity in hell with Sola mad at him.

How to win your best friend back/apologize for being a total plonker:

- *A big gesture (preferably involving food, as Sola loves food)*
- *Complete number nine on bucket list*
- *Put a plaster on bloody ear to prevent infection + early death before being able to carry out 1 and 2*

It was nearly midnight by the time Sanjeet had everything in place.

He could feel his heartbeat in his throat as he walked up to the pathway to Sola's house. He grabbed a few stones from under the hedge near the path, then climbed over the gate leading to her back garden – like he'd done so many times before – taking a deep breath before throwing the rocks at her window.

After a few attempts, a face appeared, only it wasn't the familiar heart-shaped one belonging to his best friend.

The window opened, revealing the confused

and tired face of Sola's brother, Tobi. Tobi always looked tired – Sola had told Sanjeet how she was convinced that her brother was superhuman given the amount he worked, but Sanjeet had seen the same tired look on his mum's face whenever she came back from a late shift at the hospital and he knew that Tobi was definitely human, just a human with a heavy burden to bear.

"Sanjeet?" Tobi said, eyebrows furrowing. "Why on earth…are you throwing rocks at my window?"

It was then that Sanjeet realized he'd been aiming at the wrong window. It must have been all the blood he'd lost from his ear wound, disorientating him. Or maybe it was because the end of the world was nearly upon them, and therefore the earth's axis was off-kilter, throwing him off too.

"Sorry, Tobi! The rocks weren't meant for you, they were meant for Sola," Sanjeet yelled.

This did not change the befuddled look on Tobi's face. In fact, it might have made it worse.

"Alright then…just try not to break any windows, please," Tobi said finally.

Sanjeet gave him a thumbs up and Tobi nodded before disappearing back into the house.

"Take two," Sanjeet muttered under his breath. He readied his next stone, but as he went to throw one at the *correct* window this time, he spotted the outline of a figure standing there. He blinked, finally seeing Sola's angry face appear at her open bedroom window.

He quickly grabbed the stereo he'd brought, fiddled with some of the dials and then hit play – and "You Drive Me Crazy" by Britney Spears blasted from the speakers.

It probably seemed really pathetic to onlookers – a weird boy with weird pink hair, harassing the neighbourhood with mainstream pop music – but big embarrassing gestures were necessary when it came to winning your best friend back. Especially on a day like this.

Except Sola didn't look impressed.

"*Time to bring out the big guns,*" Sanjeet whispered to himself.

He turned the music down and held up a loaf of bread he had bought from the corner shop. It was a brown sliced loaf and while Sola preferred crusty white baguettes, it was the best he could do.

Besides, Sola *loved* all bread.

Her icy expression started to melt ever so slightly.

"I'm sorry I was a dickhead earlier, and I'm sorry that I haven't been a good friend lately," he yelled. "I know the world might not end and this list might all have been for nothing, and I know you put up with so much of my bullshit, but I wanted to say that I appreciate you so much, Sola. Not being your friend is worse than the world ending," Sanjeet finished, as a light rain began to trickle down from the sky.

A part of him worried the stereo would get

damaged and his parents would kill him, but a bigger part of him didn't care.

Sanjeet watched as Sola backed away from the window. He was terrified that she actually hated him and that he'd destroyed their friendship for good. But when she reappeared at the back door that led to her kitchen, he felt a massive wave of relief.

She had her arms folded and was wearing her Mickey Mouse PJs.

"I'm sorry," Sanjeet said again. He wasn't sure what else to say.

"Okay," Sola replied, eyeing the bread. "You got me bread?"

Sanjeet nodded, then smiled sheepishly.

"I loaf you…" he said.

She laughed. "You're so gross, never say that again."

"Okay," he said.

They stared at each other for a few moments, and in those moments all he could think of was number nine on the list.

"I need to tell you something. It's something I have been meaning to say to you for a while, something I didn't think I'd ever tell anyone...let alone you," Sanjeet said, his hair plastered to his face and the dye running, staining his skin as the rain continued to fall.

Britney's voice was still murmuring quietly from the speakers.

"What is it?" Sola asked, looking a little scared.

"It's why I was acting weird earlier, when you took my bucket list... I didn't...I didn't want you to see. I wanted to tell you myself." Sanjeet looked away from her.

"You're scaring me. You're not *dying*, are you?" she asked.

This was a legitimate concern of hers. She had this fear of the people she loved most dying without her ever getting to say goodbye. It was how her mum had died – one day she was there, the next she wasn't. She never told Sola how sick she was until it was too late.

When Sola had explained her fear to Sanjeet, he'd promised to never do that to her, to tell her if anything was ever wrong with him, so they could say goodbye properly and she wouldn't be left with a permanent gaping hole in her chest like with her mum.

"N-no, I'm healthy—"

"Then what is it?"

Sola could hear people screaming in the background and see early fireworks going off. It was nearly midnight, nearly the year 2000.

Sanjeet was running out of time.

"Uh…well, you know how my dad signed me up to Boy Scouts?"

Sola nodded. "That was ages ago, you don't even go any more. What's that got to do with anything?"

Sanjeet closed his eyes. *It's okay. Just say it.* "I'm bisexual," he finally said.

"What?" Sola said, confused.

"Uh, you know how some guys like girls and some like guys? I think I like everyone—"

"I know what bisexual means, you idiot, I just don't get what Boy Scouts has to do with this?"

"Oh. I kissed a boy there when I was, like, thirteen. I think it was my sexual awakening. After it happened, I didn't know if I should tell anyone, but then today I knew I couldn't die without telling *someone*. It feels like such a big part of me, you know? And I like the idea of dying with someone knowing all of me."

Sanjeet felt a massive weight lift off his chest, though he couldn't tell what Sola was thinking. Whether she thought he was weird or not. He hoped she didn't think that he was.

"You look so ridiculous right now, holding that loaf," Sola said.

Sanjeet furrowed his eyebrows together.

"That all you have to say?" he asked.

Sola smiled. "I think I might be bisexual too.

Sometimes I look at girls and think… *Wow, she's pretty*. But I haven't actually kissed a girl before… or a guy, for that matter…so I don't know. But anyway, thank you for sharing that with me. I know it couldn't have been easy."

Sanjeet stood there in shock. This whole time, he'd pictured the worst things happening – even things he knew Sola would never do. He'd imagined Sola no longer wanting to be his friend, Sola telling everyone…but never *this*.

"You okay?" she asked.

He nodded, pushing the loaf under his arm, before taking his bucket list out of his pocket and staring at the final thing, the one that probably scared him even more than number nine.

He checked the time on his watch: a minute to midnight.

"We have a minute left," he said softly.

"We're not going to die," Sola said, squeezing his hand.

"What if we do though? What if this is it?" he asked.

"Then this is it," Sola said, smiling. "Any last words?"

Sanjeet looked at her, thinking about all the things they'd done together in their short lifetime. The school ski-trip they went on last year, where Sola had broken her foot and he'd nursed her back to health (though, in actuality, his dad had done all the cooking and nursing, he had just helped). He thought about all the times they'd stayed up watching horror films that were definitely not age-appropriate; the birthdays, the Christmases, the one million sleepovers they'd had. He thought about how many dreams Sola had appeared in, how much he thought about her, even when she wasn't around. He took in her dark skin, her braids which flowed down past her shoulders, her long lashes, her warm dark-brown eyes.

He stepped forward, dropping the loaf on the ground.

And he kissed her.

The kiss felt like it lasted for ever, even though Sola knew only a few moments had gone by in reality.

She couldn't believe this was actually happening.

Sanjeet was kissing her.

She'd imagined what this moment would be like, wondering whether it would be like in the movies, when the boy asks out the girl and they go on a romantic stroll and then he asks her to go steady and she says yes.

She never imagined they'd be moments away from catching pneumonia, or that Britney Spears would be playing, or that there'd be a soggy, sad-looking bread loaf between them.

She never imagined she'd be wearing Mickey Mouse PJs either.

But despite all of this, it somehow still felt right.

When Sanjeet finally pulled away, looking horrified by what he'd just done, he wondered if Sola hated him more than before. Whether he'd actually ruined their friendship for good by breaking a boundary that could never be unbroken.

He could barely look at her – scared that, if he did, he'd know the truth. That their friendship was officially over.

"San," Sola said, and he prepared himself for the worst.

"The time is now three minutes past twelve," she whispered.

At first, he didn't understand why she was telling him the time, but then it sank in.

"Oh."

He looked up at her and was surprised to see that there was no hatred on her face; no regret. She looked happy...*really* happy.

He looked up at the sky, wondering if there would be some sound that played to signal the end…an explosion…*something*.

But nothing came.

"Sanjeet," Sola said, and he looked back down at her.

"What?" he asked.

"I told you so," Sola said, before kissing him once again.

The End

Sanjeet's Doomsday Bucket List

1. Eat sweets for breakfast

   (this wasn't too bad, although I prefer eggs)

2. Smoke a cigarette

   (gross!!! Not worth doing ever)

3. Ride my bike without wearing a helmet

   (in hindsight, not my best decision)

4. Dye my hair pink

   (in hindsight, might be my best decision, especially seeing as Sola says it makes me look like a rockstar. Though, my mum tells me I look like a toothbrush)

5. Learn how to skateboard

   (let's never talk about this again)

6. Eat fast food *(I much prefer my mum's biryani)*

7. Have a fizzy drink *(I think I burned a hole in my oesophagus — need to get that checked out)*

8. Get a piercing

(fainting isn't fun)

9. Finally tell someone that I'm bisexual

:)

10. Tell Sola the truth *(I now have the best girlfriend in the world which is pretty cool)*

A letter from Faridah Àbíké-Íyímídé

When asked about my dreams as a child, I always gave the same answers. I would tell anyone who asked that my dream career was either a dinner lady or a writer – the former because I wanted to learn the secrets of how to make the perfect cake and custard; the latter because I loved telling stories. My dream vehicle was roller skates, especially the dangerous kind that my mum disliked. And my dream place to live was a sprawling mansion with a treehouse at the back, and in that mansion, the biggest collection of books mankind has ever seen. The problem with that final dream wasn't the fact that giant mansions tend to be extremely expensive – no, I had full confidence that I could save up and buy my unnecessarily large house. The problem was that I didn't own any books of my own and so couldn't possibly have a book collection.

I loved being able to borrow books from school and from my local library and build my own personal collection over the few days I had with the books I'd borrowed. But it always felt like temporary magic. This all changed the year I got to celebrate my first World Book Day at school. I dressed up as the character Handa from *Handa's Surprise* and went to school ready to wow all the teachers. As I suspected, they were all very impressed by my costume and I couldn't imagine that day getting any better. Except, then it did. Because at the end of the day, the teacher announced that we would all be given a voucher which would allow us to choose a book from the

World Book Day selection for free, and take it home for ever. My dream of having a massive book collection was, at last, a possibility. I could finally start my own collection of books and the magic would not be temporary.

Each year on World Book Day, I would go to school and look forward to getting another voucher and adding another book to my growing collection. And now, many years later, I have finally achieved my dream of owning a ridiculous number of books – and it all started with World Book Day.

I hope that *The Doomsday Date* can be the start of your very own collection of books and that this story about friendship, romance and, of course, the "end of the world" will perhaps inspire stories of your own. Stories that could just make it onto other people's shelves and collections too.

Faridah Àbíké-Íyímídé, February 2024

FARIDAH ÀBÍKÉ-ÍYÍMÍDÉ is the instant *New York Times*, international bestselling and award-winning author of *Ace of Spades* and *Where Sleeping Girls Lie*.

She is an avid tea drinker, a collector of strange mugs and a recent graduate from a university in the Scottish Highlands where she received a BA in English Literature. She is currently pursuing an MA in Shakespeare Studies from King's College London. When she isn't spinning dark tales, Faridah can be found examining the deeper meanings in Disney Channel original movies.

Her next novel, *Four Eids and a Funeral*, written with Adiba Jaigirdar, will be published in June 2024.

If you've enjoyed

read on for an exclusive extract
from the upcoming new romcom from
Faridah Àbíké-Íyímídé and
Adiba Jaigirdar...

FOUR EIDS

and a

FUNERAL

Faridah Àbíké-Íyímídé
&
Adiba Jaigirdar

Let's get one thing straight: this is a love story.

I know both the funeral and the fire might be alarming, but I can assure you that despite the rather unfortunate beginnings, the betrayals that would put even Shakespeare to shame, and the regrettable *incident* several Eids ago, this is simply a morbid tale about two doofuses who fell in love over the course of several years.

You may hear other iterations of this story from *untrustworthy* sources. But this is the true account of what *really* happened.

This is a tale of four Eids. And a funeral.

1

OUT OF THE BLUE

SAID

"Can Said Hossain please report to the principal's office?"

I glance up at the speaker hanging off the ceiling in the classroom, wondering if I just didn't hear correctly. But from the way Julian is looking at me with a raised eyebrow, I know that it *was* my name being called to the principal's office.

I furrow my brow at Julian. In all my time at St Francis Academy for Boys, I've never been called to the principal's office. I've never gotten into trouble. I've been so good, in fact, that I'm on honour roll, and on track for early admissions to the best universities in the country. My parents often use these facts as dinner-time conversation to impress anybody and everybody.

"Can Said Hossain please report to the principal's office *immediately*?"

Mr Thomas glances at me from his desk. "Said?" he asks, motioning towards the door. He doesn't seem too bothered about the fact that one of his top students is getting called to the principal's office out of the blue, so maybe I shouldn't be either.

Since class is almost over anyway, I gather up my things into my backpack and slip out the door. The hallways of the school are completely empty, but I can hear the sounds coming from different classrooms as I make my way down to the principal's office. The near-silence would almost be peaceful, if worry wasn't gnawing its way into my stomach.

I turn into the main office, and immediately I'm greeted by a familiar voice.

A voice that sounds a lot like my older sister's.

The closer I get, the more sure I am that it *is* her. From the fact that she's loudly trying to convince the principal that his rules are ridiculous, to her long black hair and her bright purple sweater.

"Safiyah?"

Saf turns to me, her eyes wide with…well, I'm not really sure what.

"Said!" she says. "Oh, finally. We need to go."

"What's going on?" I glance from her to Principal Walker, who has never looked so uncomfortable. Usually, he has an air of authority about him, the kind that will make any student here think twice about breaking any rules. But apparently just a few minutes with Safiyah can change all that.

"There's been an inci—" Principal Walker is cut off with a small glare from Safiyah, but my stomach drops all the same.

"Ammu? Abbu?" My mind immediately jumps to the worst possibilities.

Safiyah shakes her head slowly. "It's…Ms Barnes." And then, I just know. Even without Safiyah telling me, I know. Because I knew she was sick. I had even written to her. Sent her a get-well-soon card, like that would somehow help her deal with the cancer. But I'd never let myself consider the possibility that she might actually…

"I'm so sorry, Said." Safiyah holds out her arms, and it's like my body is working automatically. I walk into her hug. Safiyah wraps me up tightly in her warm embrace, and we stay like that for a long moment. All the while I'm trying to register it – Ms Barnes is dead. Ms Barnes, the woman who encouraged my love of reading. Without her recommendation letter, I probably wouldn't have even gotten into this school. And now she's just… gone.

"We have to go," Safiyah says as soon as I pull away from her hug. "The funeral is tomorrow morning, and if we leave now we should be able to get back to Vermont with plenty of time to spare."

"But…" I shake my head, because Safiyah's words are barely registering in my mind. Ms Barnes gone. Funeral. *Back to Vermont?*

"Said has classes," Principal Walker chimes in when I've been silent for a little too long. "There's still a whole week left until the semester is over and the summer holidays start."

Safiyah scoffs. "Look at him!" She waves her arm at me like I'm some kind of a painting in a gallery. I blink at Principal Walker, because, really, I'm not sure what he's supposed to be looking at. "You think he's going to be okay going through classes for another whole week? He needs to be back home, with his family. He's distraught."

"This Ms Barnes was…a family member?" Principal Walker asks.

Safiyah glares at him once more. "Is he only allowed to be upset when a family member passes?" she asks. Her voice doesn't rise – Safiyah doesn't shout – but there's this way she has of making it all low and scary. When we were kids, Safiyah used to use this voice to make me do all the chores she didn't want to do. I've grown immune to it now – a little bit immune, at least. But Principal Walker is obviously meeting Safiyah for the first time. He shifts uncomfortably in his seat.

"Well, no. It's just, we don't know a Ms Barnes, and—"

"Check his school records. You'll find Ms Barnes's letter of recommendation for Said. They were close. She was like a mentor to him."

Was. That's the word that echoes in my head over and over again. Ms Barnes *was* like a mentor. Because she is no more.

"I just don't know if—"

"We're going!" Safiyah exclaims, throwing her hand up. "I'm taking Said, and we're packing up his things and driving back to Vermont, whether you think his loss is important enough to warrant missing a week of classes or not." She spins around and stomps out the door.

I stand there for a moment longer, because in her anger she's obviously forgotten that she came here to get me.

Principal Walker heaves a sigh. "Said, you can go. I'll send a message to the registration office," he says. "And I'm...sorry for your loss."

I swallow the lump in my throat. "Thank you," I say.

Safiyah seems completely unimpressed by my dorm. Of course, my side of the room is perfectly intact. Everything in its place, and a place for everything. But Julian's side is a completely different matter. There are clothes strewn all over, and his books are anywhere *but* on the little shelf above each of our desks specifically designated for our schoolbooks.

"How does Julian ever find anything in this pigsty?" Safiyah asks, clicking her tongue with disapproval as she eyes his side of the room.

"He gets by," I say, while staring at my own side of the room. I figured I still had an entire week left to pack up for the summer. Now, with grief lodged in my throat like a rock, the idea of putting away all my things seems even more daunting.

Safiyah seems to almost sense this, because she slips past me and begins pulling clothes from my drawers and into an open suitcase.

"When did it happen?" I ask, after a moment.

Safiyah looks up at me, but she doesn't stop in her one-track focus of packing up my things. "I'm not sure. A few days ago, I think."

A few days ago. Shouldn't I have known something was wrong? Isn't there something in the universe that's supposed to tell you when someone you love is suffering? Is…dead? But for the past few days, I went about my life like everything was normal. I went to my classes, played soccer with Julian, did my homework. All the while, Ms Barnes was gone.

"How did you find out?" I ask Safiyah, instead of indulging my guilt for longer. I can feel the pressure in my throat growing, can feel the pinprick of tears behind my eyes. I'm definitely not going to break down in front of Safiyah like this. Not now.

Safiyah stops in her tracks for a moment. "Um, I just…someone from home told me." She goes back to packing up my things like she didn't hesitate to answer my question. But I immediately know: it must have been *her* – Tiwa. For all her faults (and she has many), Tiwa, at least, loved Ms Barnes as much as I do. At one point in our lives, Tiwa would have told me as soon as she knew.

"Okay, all done!" Safiyah says, zipping up the suitcase. "The sooner we get out of here, the sooner we can get to…well, the funeral." She glances at me out of the corner of her eye, and there's sympathy written all over her face. She's looking at me like I'm about to break, or something.

I duck my head and approach Julian's unkempt desk. "I should let Julian know," I say. "He'll wonder…what's happened."

"Can't you just text him or something?" Safiyah asks.

I shake my head, picking up a pen from his desk and unfurling a balled-up piece of paper. "We can't check our phones in between classes. When he gets to our room, he'll be confused."

"Well, I'm going to get your things into the car," Safiyah says, dragging my suitcase behind her. "So, I'll see you there in a few minutes, okay?"

"Okay."

"Don't forget to add a Pokémon drawing to your note," Safiyah adds as an afterthought.

I pause. "How do you know Julian likes Pokémon?"

Safiyah just glances pointedly at the dozens of

Pokémon plushies lined up on Julian's bed. "Every time I've spoken to him, he mentions Pokémon half a dozen times," she says before slipping out the door, and I realize she has a point.

With Safiyah gone, the rock in my throat seems to grow even larger. I swallow down the lump and tap my pen against the piece of paper. How do I explain to Julian exactly what's happened, when he doesn't know anything about Ms Barnes?

I had to leave in a hurry because my hometown librarian passed away? But Ms Barnes was so much more than that. She was my friend, my confidante.

My sister came to drive me back to Vermont early, I scribble down quickly, *because…* I stop there, unsure of what to say next. *Because a friend of mine passed away.* It doesn't seem like enough, but I guess it's all the information Julian needs. *I'll see you over the holidays,* I add, and do a quick doodle of Psyduck, which is – for some strange reason – his favourite Pokémon. And just that two-minute drawing lets a strange relief wash over me. Like learning about Ms Barnes's death had twisted me into a knot of grief, and the ink against the paper was letting some of that grief out.

"You should cry," Safiyah says once we've been on the road for a few hours. There's been nothing keeping us company except for whatever radio station gets picked up by the car's frequency. We've listened to everything from country music to heavy metal, and even a talk show about different kinds of potatoes.

"Why would I cry?" I ask.

"Well, because crying is good for you. You shouldn't keep your emotions bottled up like this."

I roll my eyes and stare out my side of the window instead of looking at Safiyah. Ever since she started majoring in psychology at college, she thinks she knows everything. Well, she's always been like this, but it's just worse now because she has the promise of an undergraduate degree to back up her know-it-all attitude.

"Said…I'm sorry," Safiyah says softly after a moment. And I thaw a little. She's trying to help – even if she's being completely and utterly unhelpful.

"I'm fine," I say, even as pressure builds behind my eyes. I blink away the tears and keep my eyes trained on the window.

"You should share a happy memory you have of Ms Barnes," Safiyah says. "She would like that, right?"

Safiyah didn't really know Ms Barnes, but she's right. She *would* like that. Ms Barnes was the kind of person who liked to think about the positive things in life. She wouldn't want me to spend this entire drive glaring out my window, being annoyed at my sister, and feeling guilty because I didn't write to her enough during her time at the hospital.

I try to think of a happy memory. "Well, I remember when I got into St Francis, and Tiwa was annoyed at me. She said she wouldn't speak to me ever again if I decided to go."

"That *doesn't* sound like a happy memory…"

"Let me finish," I say. "She was so annoyed at me. But then she went to see Ms Barnes. She said Ms Barnes invited Tiwa into her office, and made her tea in her little china cups. That's what she did when she wanted to have a serious conversation. And she told Tiwa about how she had written the letter of recommendation for me, and all the reasons why I needed to go to St Francis, and all the ways it would help me. And Tiwa was still annoyed, but when she came to our house afterwards, she understood. She wanted me to go."

"That's a story about Ms Barnes? It sounds like it's more about Tiwa," Safiyah says.

I scowl at Safiyah but I know there's some truth to what she's saying.

The thing is, every happy memory of Ms Barnes somehow feels tied to Tiwa. Even every happy

memory of home is tied to her. "It's just that…
that's the kind of person Ms Barnes was. She was
always making peace between me and Tiwa, always
helping us see each other's side. I thought Tiwa
would be angry at me the whole week before I left
for St Francis, but Ms Barnes made sure that didn't
happen. She made sure I had the best last week in
New Crosshaven."

Because of Ms Barnes, I knew that even though
I was leaving, I would always have people back
home. I would always have Tiwa. I would always
have Ms Barnes. But Tiwa and I aren't friends any
more. And Ms Barnes is gone. I don't get a lot of
time to think about that, though, because the next
moment, Safiyah swerves the car so fast that I'm
pretty sure I see my entire life flash before my eyes.
A car honks in front of us, and misses us by just a
few seconds.

Safiyah curses under her breath, and I turn to
her with a glare.

"What the hell was that? You could have gotten us killed."

"It's dark," she says. "I didn't see that car coming. It's fine, it'll be fine."

I pinch the bridge of my nose with my fingers. I always knew Safiyah was a terrible driver, but I didn't realize how much worse she might be at night. I check my phone for the time. It's already ten p.m., and we haven't even left Virginia yet. It'll probably be a few more hours until we're in Vermont.

"I think we should pull over for the night. Get some rest somewhere."

"We'll be late to the funeral!" Safiyah says. "It's just a few more hours."

"You're tired," I say. "You've been driving for hours. You want it to be our funeral next?"

Safiyah sighs. "Okay, fine. We'll find a place to stay for the night, but…we'll have to be up at the crack of dawn if we want to make it back in time."

I nod, already setting multiple alarms on my phone. There's no way that I'm going to miss my chance to say goodbye to Ms Barnes. Not even Safiyah's terrible driving can keep me away.

2

WHAT AN ASSHOLE

Tiwa

Funerals to me are like weddings.

People fly out from far and wide to celebrate someone's life. There's food, music and family drama – only, after a wedding is over, the guests don't dig up a six-foot hole and shove the celebrant in.

I guess that's the only difference.

That and the fact that at least at a funeral, it's acceptable to be dressed in all black and to wear an unflattering scowl all day.

Do that at your auntie Amaal's wedding and suddenly you're the weird one. At a funeral, there's little judgement. I guess everyone is too busy being sad to judge others and how they look.

Besides, it's not what Ms Barnes would have wanted. She was all for being yourself and not giving a crap about what anyone thought of you. She would have wanted everyone to show up here as their authentic selves, whether that be wearing a circus costume or a fancy suit and tie. She'd want to know everyone was celebrating her life without forcing themselves to be less than they are.

When Ms B got her cancer diagnosis last year and had to start chemo, I remember how she'd bought these ridiculous wigs and would wear them without a care in the world. Her favourite was this electric-blue one that kind of reminded me of the wig from that old Katy Perry music video. She'd worn that wig everywhere she could: to my birthday, to the annual New Crosshaven pumpkin festival, and even to the Eid party at my house last year.

Picture after picture of her with her big smile and her bright-blue hair is on the board by the entrance of the funeral home, where everyone has hung up their favourite memories of her.

A stark contrast from the way I imagine she looks now inside the closed wooden casket: her eyes shut, her face pale, and her head mostly bald with small tufts of unruly ginger locks, like it usually was when she wasn't wearing her wigs.

No more smiles, no more telling me funny stories from her youth, no more life.

No more Ms B.

I wipe my eyes with the back of my hand and reach out to touch the casket's lid, hoping that when I do it will somehow trigger something in the universe and I'll wake up and this will all have been a really messed-up dream.

But of course, when I touch it, nothing happens.

I'm still here in this funeral home.

And Ms Barnes is still dead.

Someone clears their throat. When I look up, I'm met with an annoyed-looking stranger peering down at me.

"Are you done? You've been standing here for ten minutes. Other people want to pay respects too," he says.

I now notice the long line behind him. I didn't realize I've been here for so long.

"Oh…s-sorry," I say, swallowing the knot at the back of my throat. It wouldn't help anyone if I started crying in front of this stranger, who's already pissed off at me.

I wipe my eyes again and give Ms B one final glance, before moving away from the casket.

The room is crowded, filled with people from all over, young and old. A lot of people must have really loved the library – or just Ms B. She had an infectious personality that made it hard not to want to hang around her all the time.

I recognize a few people from school. But no

one I'm friendly enough with to strike up a conversation or even give a polite nod to. So I decide to find my own corner.

It's weird to think that I was in this very same funeral home less than two years ago, and yet everything and nothing has changed. The layout is different, as is the paint on the walls, once an oatmeal beige, now a sickly green. The feelings that come with being here have stayed the same, though. I still feel the same squeezing in my chest, the same pit in my stomach, the same urge to hide from the reality of things.

There are seats all around the room, most unoccupied. There is something about standing at a funeral that makes the whole thing less depressing. Sitting forces you to think, which I guess is the last thing I want to do right now. So when I finally find my seat, I do what anyone does when they want to avoid dealing with their thoughts and emotions: I take my phone out and turn it on. I'm hoping that while I've been here all morning, something scandalous happened online to some rich celebrity that will take all my attention away.

When my phone switches on, I'm immediately met by four missed calls from my best friend, Safiyah.

I sit up, eyebrows furrowing. Saf usually never calls so early.

I hope everything is okay with her... I press the call back button just as the room falls silent.

Saf's familiar ringtone sounds somewhere in the room: the shrill sound of *The Powerpuff Girls* theme song.

But it wouldn't make sense for Safiyah to be here; she barely knew Ms B. Maybe there's another person with Saf's level of love for the Powerpuff Girls. But that's impossible.

I look up, noticing now how almost everyone in the room is staring in the same direction. At the front entrance.

Strange.

I stand to get a better view, regretting my decision when I see what, or rather who, had caught everyone's attention.

My best friend, Safiyah Hossain, and her brother, Said.

I take back what I said about not being judgemental at a funeral. People are definitely judging. They both look incredibly out of place here.

Safiyah is wearing a bright purple sweater with a print that says *Hello Suckers* in bold and Said... well, he's wearing his fancy boarding school uniform. Looking like his usual douchebag self.

Safiyah spots me and smiles, waving frantically as though we aren't at a funeral. Some people turn to look at me now.

I hesitate before I walk over to her, grimacing when I accidentally lock eyes with Said for a brief moment.

When I get to the entrance, Saf pulls me in for a tight hug.

"I missed you so much, T. How've you been?" Saf asks when she finally frees me, as though we don't talk every single day.

She has this creepy serial killer smile on her face. It's weirding me out.

"Uh…I'm okay, considering," I say.

Saf nods, looking sad.

"I can imagine how hard it's been. I know you both really liked her," she says.

The *both* she is referring to is me and Said.

I'm almost forced to look at him now. It would be weird if I didn't.

When I do, I'm surprised to see him staring right back. Even more surprising, though, is the expression on his face. His usual disdain whenever we're together is replaced by something new.

His eyes are bloodshot and glassy – he looks like he's been…*crying.*

But I don't understand why when he was perfectly fine going off to boarding school and abandoning everyone he knew. He was fine ignoring all of Ms B's emails. And when she told him she was dying, he had nothing to say about that either.

Why pretend to care now?

It's too late.

I'm still staring at him when he finally opens his mouth to speak.

"I'm going to go and pay my respects," Said says, turning to Saf now.

She squeezes his hand and pats his back, and he moves past me like he always does these days. Like I'm invisible.

I roll my eyes. *That's* the Said I know and hate.

"What an asshole," I mutter, forgetting Safiyah is here. I usually try to keep my thoughts about her brother to myself when she's around.

"I'm sorry, I tried calling earlier to give you a

heads-up," Saf says, looking guilty.

I shake my head. "It's okay. Besides, he'll only be here for a day or two as usual. I'm just so happy to see you," I tell her, but the guilt still hasn't left her face.

"About that—"

"Hi, everyone! Can I have your attention please – the wake will be in the community centre. We're all about to head over, so please grab your things and get ready to leave," Clara Sheppard, one of the librarians who worked with Ms Barnes, announces to the crowd.

"We should leave quickly before the road gets busy," I say.

"Let me just go and get Said first, okay?" Saf replies.

I nod, trying to mask my displeasure at the sound of his name. I guess this is the cost of having my best friend be the older sister of my sworn enemy.

Saf reappears a few moments later with Said. We stare at each other again in silence, my arms folded now to show how displeased I am with having him here.

His glowering tells me he feels the same.

Safiyah clears her throat. "So! The community centre…I take it I'm driving?"

"I don't mind driving," I say, mostly because I'd rather not die today. Saf drives like she's in a video game and has an unlimited number of lives.

"You sure?" Saf asks.

I nod. Very sure.

I glance at Said, again, expecting a protest. But it doesn't come.

Saf nudges him and he looks at me, still scowling.

"Tiwa," he says with a nod.

I raise an eyebrow. Is that meant to be a greeting?

"Said," I reply in the same weird, antisocial manner. He's usually a lot more vocal, but I guess since his favourite childhood librarian died, he might not have much to say after all.

"Tell Tiwa I'll be walking to the community centre. Don't want to be the last ones to arrive there with the snail's pace she goes at. I'll see you in a few," he says to Saf.

Clearly Said doesn't realize I have his time today. After all, other than crying about the person you used to know, now dead and lying back in a casket, funerals are relatively uneventful.

"That's rich coming from the guy weeping at the funeral of the woman he spent the past four years ignoring. Hope you have a lovely walk. With any luck a coyote might eat you on the way and you'll never have to be put through the misery of being driven by me again," I say.

Said turns red, but his expression is unreadable.

"Seriously, guys, we will get kicked out, our slot is over," Clara says, clapping her hands together and gesturing towards the door.

"You're such a—" Said begins, but stops himself at the last second, as though scared that the ghost of Ms B will rise up and reprimand him.

I smile, victorious. Which only makes him look more murderous.

"That's it, I'm driving. And you're both going to sit in the back seat and not complain about it or each other. Got it?" Safiyah asks.

We both stay silent.

"Good, now hurry up. I have plans after this," she adds.

"Plans? Ishra plans?" I ask, saying the second part slowly.

Ishra is a girl who works in the community centre and has been the target of Safiyah's flirtations for years. It became a running joke among us, the one-sided crush she had on her, until recently, when Ishra started flirting back.

Saf smiles, before walking out the door without confirming or denying anything.

I'll dig for more information later when Said isn't around.

Once we get into the car, I do what I usually do whenever I'm about to experience Saf's driving. I pray that Allah protects us against any scars or permanent injuries incurred from this.

When I'm done, I face the other way. I look out the window, trying to ignore Said's close proximity to me, and the stuff I couldn't help but notice in the short glances I got earlier. Like how much taller he's gotten, and how his hair is longer and floppier, and how my stomach turns every time he glances my way.

Like now.

I ignore all of that and focus on my second round of prayers, pleading to God once again that Safiyah doesn't kill us all today.

Enemies, friends...or something more?
Find out what happens with
Said and Tiwa in

FOUR
EIDS
and a
FUNERAL

Faridah Àbíké-Íyímídé
&
Adiba Jaigirdar

COMING JUNE 2024

Let's get one thing straight: this is a love story.

Said Hossain hates Tiwa Olatunji. And Tiwa would happily
never see Said again in her life. Growing up, the two were
inseparable, but they have barely spoken since the incident
many Eids ago and both of them would like to keep it that
way. But when Said comes home for a funeral and the town's
Islamic Centre burns down on the same day, they have to
face each other again and sparks fly.

Both of them want to see the Islamic Centre rebuilt. For
Tiwa, it represents the community that she loves and a way
to keep her fractured family together. For Said, it's an
opportunity to build his portfolio for his secret application to
art school, where he hopes that he'll be able to pursue his
dreams of becoming an artist, rather than a doctor.

Working with your sworn enemy is never easy, and this
could be the hardest thing that Said and Tiwa have ever
done. But in trying to save the Islamic Centre and Eid, could
these enemies become something else…?

A gorgeous, bright and swoony YA rom-com from two
bestselling, award-winning stars of YA:
Faridah Àbíké-Íyímídé and Adiba Jaigirdar

Also by FARIDAH ÀBÍKÉ-ÍYÍMÍDÉ

AN INSTANT NEW YORK TIMES BESTSELLER

WINNER OF THE 2021 BOOKS ARE MY BAG READERS'
AWARD FOR YOUNG ADULT FICTION

SHORTLISTED FOR THE YA BOOK PRIZE
SHORTLISTED FOR THE DIVERSE BOOK AWARDS

Hello, Niveus High. It's me. Who am I? That's not important. All you need to know is...I'm here to divide and conquer. – Aces

Welcome to Niveus Private Academy, where money paves the hallways, and the students are never less than perfect. Until now. Because anonymous texter, Aces, is bringing two students' dark secrets to life.

Talented musician Devon buries himself in rehearsals, but he can't escape the spotlight when his private photos go public.

Head girl Chiamaka isn't afraid to get what she wants, but soon everyone will know the price she has paid for power.

Someone is out to get them both. Someone who holds all the aces. And they're planning much more than a high-school game...

ACE OF SPADES is *Gossip Girl* meets *Get Out*; an incendiary and utterly compelling thriller with a shocking twist that delves deep into the heart of institutionalized racism.

"Tense, compelling YA thriller that will appeal to fans of Karen M. McManus." *The Guardian*

Bestselling author of Ace of Spades

FARIDAH
ÀBÍKÉ-ÍYÍMÍDÉ

WHERE
SLEEPING
GIRLS LIE

Secrets haunt these hallowed halls

This was a mistake, the voice in her head whispered.
You should never have come…

Sade Hussein is the new girl at the prestigious Alfred Nobel Academy. She has no idea what to expect of her mysterious new boarding school – an institution steeped in tradition and secrets. But she certainly didn't imagine her roommate, Elizabeth, to go missing on her first night. Or for people to think Sade had something to do with it.

Suddenly everyone is talking about Sade, including the Unholy Trinity: the three most popular girls at school. Swept up in their circle, Sade can't shake the sense that there's more to Elizabeth's disappearance – especially as the teachers don't seem to care.

And then a student is found dead.

It's clear there's more to Alfred Nobel Academy and its students than Sade could have imagined – and she must race to uncover the truth. But secrets lurk around every corner and beneath every surface…secrets that rival even her own.

COMING 14th MARCH 2024

HAPPY WORLD BOOK DAY!

Choosing to read in your spare time can make you happier and more successful. We want that for every young person.

NOW YOU'VE READ THIS BOOK YOU COULD:

• Swap it • Read it again • Recommend it to a friend • Talk about it

WHERE WILL YOUR READING JOURNEY TAKE YOU NEXT?

Why not challenge a friend, teacher, local bookseller or librarian to recommend your next read based on your interests?

 Find your **LOCAL LIBRARY** ⫷⫷

Find your **NEAREST BOOKSELLER** ⫸⫸

START A BOOK RECOMMENDATION CHAT!

• I really liked... (What should I read next?)
• I like books that have... (character types, plot types)
• I would like to try... (genre or non-fiction or poetry)
...can you recommend a good place to start?
• I am interested in...

Changing lives through a love of books and reading.

World Book Day® is a charity sponsored by National Book Tokens

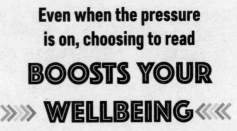

Even when the pressure is on, choosing to read

BOOSTS YOUR

»»» WELLBEING «««

Make a **READING HABIT** - try scheduling 10 minutes a day

Choose your **READING** to match your **MOOD**

Hide distractions to find **YOUR FOCUS**

GET READY - take a breath or two

MIX IT UP - try an audiobook on a walk

SOCIALISE - chat about it, read together or join a book club

DISCOVER your next read at **WORLDBOOKDAY.COM**

Look out for more
unforgettable reads from
Faridah Àbíké-Íyímídé,
coming soon...